D1577090

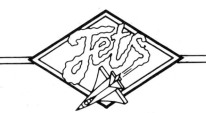

The Fizziness Business

Business

Robin Kingsland

A & C Black · London

Published 1990 by A & C Black (Publishers) Ltd
35 Bedford Row, London WC1R 4JH

Reprinted 1994
Copyright © 1990 Robin Kingsland

ISBN 0–7136–3244–5

A CIP catalogue record for this book
is available from the British Library

Filmset by Kalligraphic Design Ltd, Horley, Surrey
Printed in Great Britain by William Clowes Ltd, Beccles and London

Chapter One

Oswald Bingly, alias Prisoner 45863, was hard at work in the prison kitchen. The guards watching him were very impressed. Oswald seemed to be settling into the prison routine at last.

But what they didn't know was that Oswald was thinking . . .

Dastardly thoughts of ESCAPE!

Meanwhile . . .

On the other side of the prison, Oswald's cell mate Stig Stubble was looking very shifty and suspicious as he stitched mailbags. But what his guards did not know was that Stig Stubble was thinking . . .

Nothing.

Absolutely nothing at all.

Not a solitary sausage.

A Solitary Sausage ➤

But then, that was Stig all over.

4

Chapter Two

When they got back to the cell that night, Oswald was still thinking. Being a criminal mastermind involves a lot of thinking. Oswald was always dreaming up some plot, or plan, or scheme, or swindle. And when he wasn't doing that, he had mean thoughts – just for practice.

But this time, Oswald was planning

an ESCAPE!

This was to be Oswald's and Stig's second escape attempt. The first one, need I say, had not been successful – but then, the first one had been thought up by Stig's mum.

Mrs Stubble had sent 'her boys' a cake. Hidden inside were:

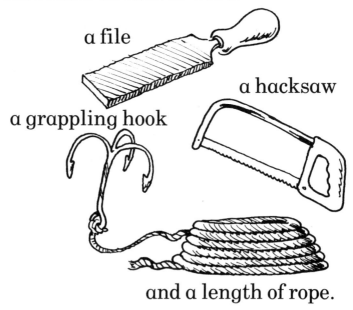

a file

a hacksaw

a grappling hook

and a length of rope.

All the sort of stuff you need to break out of prison.

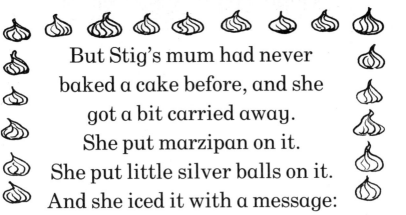

But Stig's mum had never baked a cake before, and she got a bit carried away.
She put marzipan on it.
She put little silver balls on it.
And she iced it with a message:

Good luck, with the Breakout!

love from Mumsy

The guards got the cake.

Stig and Oswald got two weeks confined to their cells.

Ever since the cake catastrophe, Oswald had been trying to come up with another plan. Stig came up with one every day, but they were usually clumsy, or impractical, or both. For instance there was:

Stig Stubble's TUNNEL PLAN

Stig had come up with this plan in the mailbag workshop. He would steal a needle, and smuggle it up to the cell. Then . . .

10

Stig showed his plan to Oswald.

'We'll follow *my* plan,' said Oswald.
Stig looked puzzled. He often did.
'I didn't know you had one, boss.'
'I haven't yet,' said Oswald, 'but
whatever I come up with is bound to
be better than your puny efforts!'

Sure enough, he hatched an
ambitious and dastardly scheme.

Chapter Three

Oswald had been developing two very special recipes in the prison kitchen:

One was for custard.

Oswald's Mustard Custard was vile, but more important than that, it had a skin so rubbery that a hatchet swung by a strongman ⟹

would simply . . .

. . . bounce off it!

The other recipe was for a drink:

14

Super Fizz is so **GASSY** it can inflate a rubber dingy to the size of an **Aircraft Carrier!** and send it floating off into space.

Super Fizz!

These two recipes were to be Oswald's tools in his Great Escape.

For three days, Oswald smuggled custard skin up to the cell. And night after night, by the light of a greasy candle —

Stig stitched them together.

Then, the fateful day arrived.

Chapter Four

Oswald decided to make his move during exercise period.

If the guards had paid close attention, they might have noticed that one of the prisoners was 'clinking' slightly . . .

. . . while another looked even fatter than usual.

As soon as the guards turned away,
Stig pulled from his jacket a great
flollopping mass of sewn together
custard skins. At the same time,
Oswald produced a bottle of
SuperFizz and . . .

The custard skin began to grow . . .

and grow . . .

and grow .

The custard contraption rose
uncertainly into the air, and lifted
the two jailbirds up

   . . . and up . . .

Alarms sounded, and
guards ran forward, but

they

       were

too

     late.

They watched, helpless, as Oswald
Bingly and Stig Stubble floated
majestically over the wall
to freedom.

Chapter Five

They floated for some time.

Then, when Oswald was sure that they weren't being followed,

Very well, Stubble. You may bring us down.

And so

JAB!

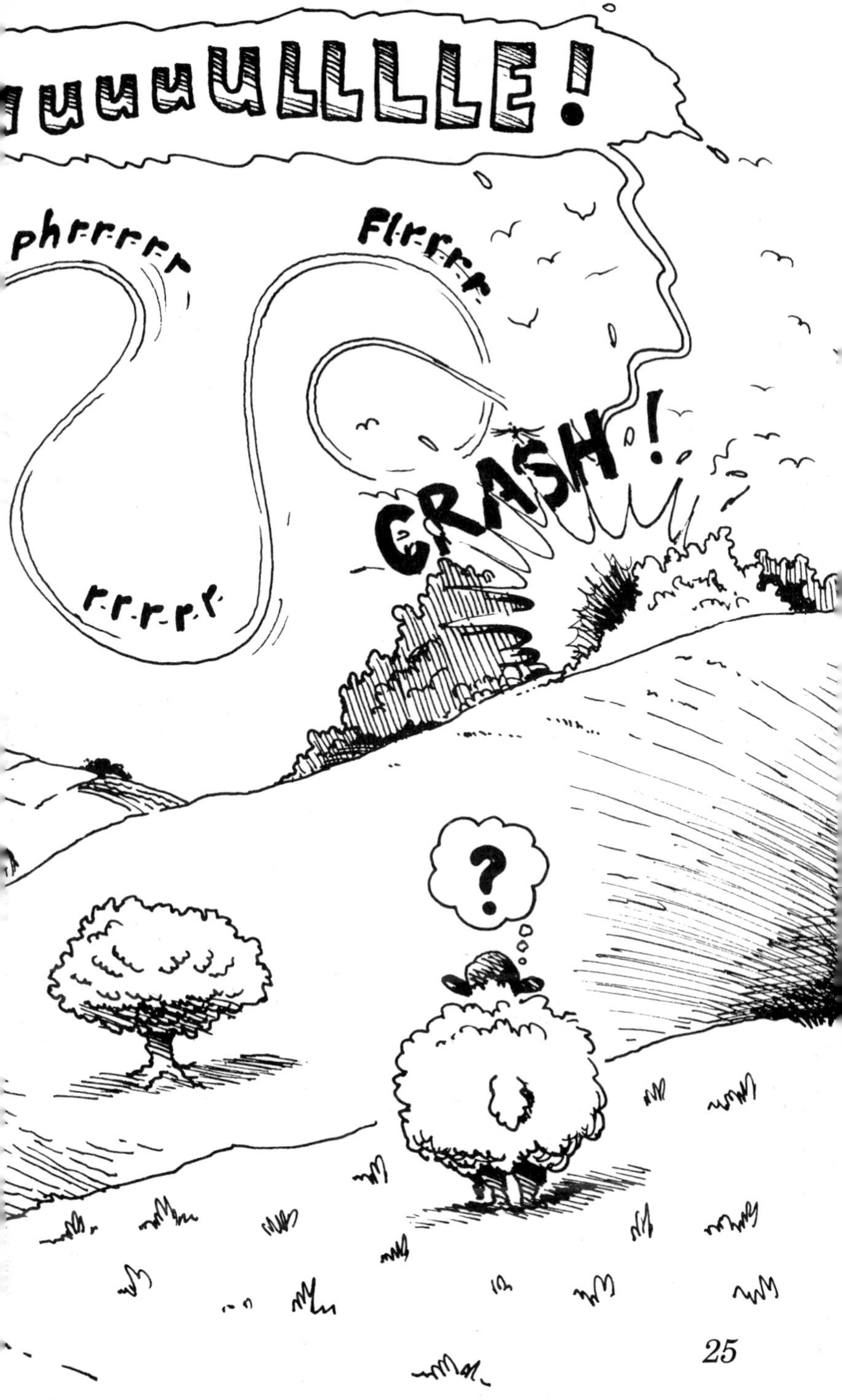
uuuuULLLLE!
phrrrrrr
Flrrrrr
rrrrrr
CRASH!
?

The first thing the two crooks
needed was somewhere to hide.
They set about building a shelter

– at least, Stig did . . .

Stig was just putting the finishing
touches to the hideout, when:

Oswald leaped out of his hammock,
waving his newspaper.

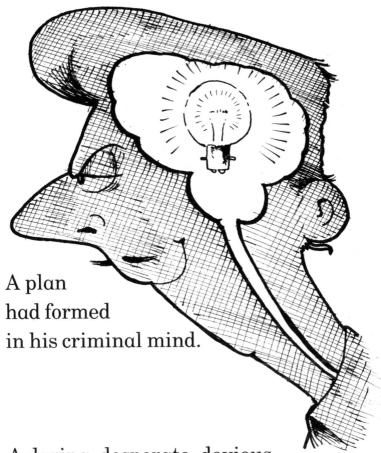

A plan
had formed
in his criminal mind.

A daring, desperate, devious,
devilish plan, which he dreamed up
while reading the article on page *14*
of the newspaper.

U F O SPOTTED

A local man was seeing psychiatrists today, after claiming to see a U.F.O.

"It was big and round," said Mr Brian Tube, 43, "It was custard coloured, and there were two martians dangling from it — one tall skinny one, and one fat ugly one."

A spokesman for the family said that Mr Tube had been overworking.

A spokesman for the Insta-Call Cab Company said "You've got the wrong number—you want the U.F.O Spotters, next door"

Mr Brian Tube

BAFFLING ESCAPE:

Prison warders were baffled yesterday when two prisoners escaped.

Prison warder, Alf Grubb said "I am baffled". A colleague later added "Me too."

CROWN JEWELS ON THE MOVE!

The Tower of London, home of the Royal Crown Jewels of Britain, today announced that the Jewels are being put away for a while.

The Jewels are usually kept guarded in the basement of the Tower, where the public can see them.

The Crown J

However, while drains in the basement are unblocked, the Jewels are being kept in another room.

A spokesman for the Tower of London said

"I can't tell you where we are keeping them. After all, we wouldn't want to have them stolen, would we? Ha Ha".

'Stubble,' Oswald said, 'You and I are going to do the *BIG* one. We are going to steal *THE CROWN JEWELS!*'

Stig thought for a second. 'Is that the pub in Whippet Lane?'

'No you idiot!' snapped Oswald. 'I'm talking about *the* Crown Jewels. The Queen's sparklers!'

Oswald explained the plan. It was long, and complicated, and Stig didn't understand all of it. Actually he didn't understand *any* of it, but by cracky, it sounded impressive.

'Of course,' said Oswald, 'We'll need an accomplice.'

'That's why I'm sending for:

"Jimmy the Crow."

Jimmy the Crow?

Now Stig knew a lot of criminals.

Bed-stead Fred

Harry the Weasel

Georgia the Forger

Shifty Shirley

Benny the Fence

But he'd never heard of
Jimmy the Crow.
'Why do they call him that then?'
he asked.

'Because his name is James . . .

and he's a crow!'

Stig Stubble didn't like Jimmy the Crow from the start. For one thing, he found it difficult to like something that lived on a perch, fed on worms but was still ten times cleverer than him. But it wasn't just that. Jimmy the crow was rude, and scruffy, and smelled slightly.

Just like Stig, in fact.

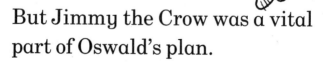

Who are you calling 'Scruffy,' Potato-face?

But Jimmy the Crow was a vital part of Oswald's plan.

34

If you go to the Tower of London, you notice something straight away.

There are

ravens

everywhere.

No one would notice one more – even if this one was spying through windows and making notes.

There was one tiny problem. Jimmy the Crow was not a raven. But Oswald Bingly was not a man to let that stand in his way.

Chapter Six

Oswald had been swotting up on Crows and Ravens. He had noticed two main differences.

1. Ravens have good manners.

If a crow sees a worm this will happen:

If a raven sees a worm, this will happen:

Which brings us to the second difference.

2. Ravens are thinner than Crows.

After all, how many worms would volunteer to be eaten?

None, that's how many!

So, before he could send Jimmy off to spy, Oswald had to spend days teaching him to 'talk posh'.

Howww Nowww, Browwwn CAW!

No, No, NO!!

And being fat, even by crow standards, he had to wear a corset.

At last, after weeks of work, Jimmu the crow became . . .

Top Hole!

Frightful!

Whacko!

Well Played Sah!

Felix the Raven

Jimmy flew off

Rum do!

good show!

=FRAP=

=FRRAP=

to the
Tower of
London

to spy . . . =FRAP=

=FRAP=

While Stig and Oswald got ready to
play their parts.

Chapter Seven

The big day got nearer, and Stig
worked hard to make disguises.
It was taking
a little longer
than planned.

Stubble, we're stealing the Crown Jewels, not running in a **Sack race!**

Sorry boss. I've only done mail-bags before.

Finally, though, everything was
ready. Stig and Oswald were now
disguised as . . .

And the next day, they joined the queue outside

Chapter Eight

'Oswaline' and 'Stigwell' wandered around the Tower of London. You would have thought that they were ordinary American tourists – unless you had seen inside Oswaline's handbag.

Bag for Jewels

Superfizz

Sweets

Ultra-Gummy Custard pies

Ball of String

Custard Balloon

Through the rooms they went, pretending to be interested in everything. Then they reached the jewel room.

On the door was a notice.

Oswald gave Stig a withering look.
'When we are rich, Stubble,' he said,
'I'm going to buy you a brain.'

Then he looked around for one of
the famous Beefeater guards.

Algy, the famous Beefeater guard,
was just coming
round the corner.
Oswald tapped him
on the shoulder and,
in a truly awful American
accent, said,

Could you show us to where your
wonderful Crown Jewels are
being kept, please?

No. Sorry, madam,
but that would be
more than my
job's worth.

Oswald took a deep breath and
WAILED.

The sobbing
went on
and on
and on.

If there was an award for 'the best
performance in a pack of lies'
Oswald would have won it,
hands down.

Algy the Beefeater tried to stay
calm, but 'Oswaline' just would not
stop crying. Algy got

more

and more

and more

embarrassed.

Oswald's performance was so good
that in the end Stig began to cry
too. Even Algy had to
blow his
nose.

Pulling himself together, Algy said
'I suppose one little look can't do
any harm.'

Oswald looked up and fluttered
his eyelashes so hard that
one of them fell off.
Algy gallantly
picked it up.

'If you'll just follow me, madam,' he said, 'I'll see what I can do.'

Algy the Beefeater led the odd little procession through corridors, up stairs, along passages and through low wooden doors. Then they reached a steep spiral staircase. ⇒

and then the top way up to all the crooks

Algy led the two

Algy opened a door, and there they were – Stig and Oswald drooled over millions of pounds worth of spangle and shine, twinkle and glitz, sparkle and gleam.

'Ready Stubble?' whispered Oswald.

Oswald launched into the next part of his plan.

And he swooned . .

dramatically.

Algy rushed to help. But suddenly Oswald leaped up. His hands were full of Ultra Gummy Custard tarts.

After that everything happened very quickly.

While Stig
tied Algy,
Oswald
ran to the
window and
whistled.

Jimmy the Crow swooped in and
took up his position, as lookout
outside the door.

All clear
Ozzie!

Stig
and Oswald
stuffed a bag with jewels.
Then Oswald snapped
'Custard Balloon!'

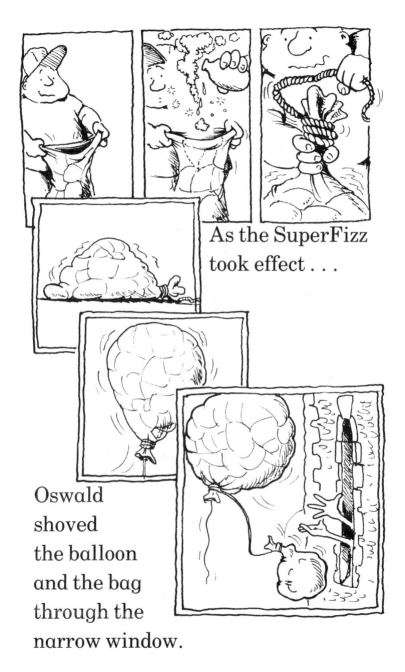

As the SuperFizz
took effect . . .

Oswald
shoved
the balloon
and the bag
through the
narrow window.

Jimmy the Crow flapped out scruffily after the loot.

Oswald breathed a sigh of relief. He had pulled off the crime of the century, and he had done it in three and a quarter minutes.

The loot was bobbing safely across London, so all that he and Stig had to do was walk out – two innocent American tourists – it was so simple, it was brilliant.

Chapter Nine

Stig, too, was simple. But not, alas, brilliant! He was thirsty though. It was hot work stealing the crown jewels. So when his eye fell on the spare bottle of SuperFizz he thought 'Just the job'.

But it was too late! There was a

Stig's stomach sounded like demented hot water pipes.

Then he began to

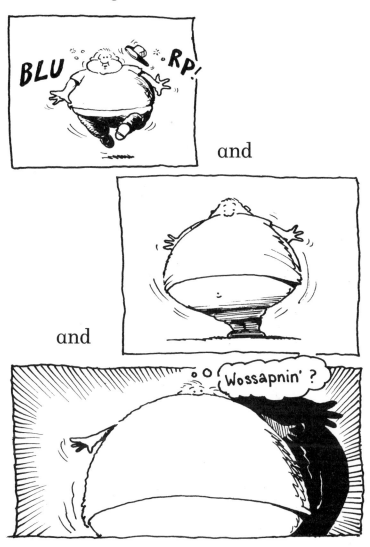

and

and

Panicking, Oswald tried to frogmarch Stig to the door.

It was the worst thing he could have done. Just as Oswald got Stig into the narrow doorway of the jewel room, there was a final, volcanic rumble, and Stig stuck . . .

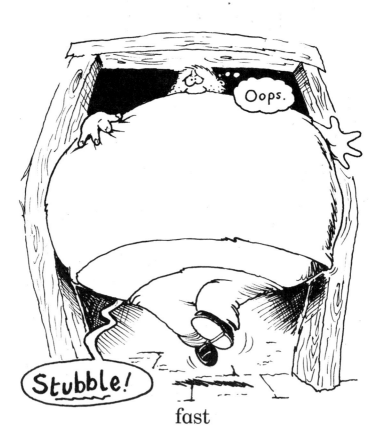

fast

No amount
of pushing,

or pulling

or pummelling
could get him
out of the
way.

No amount of wriggling or squirming could get Oswald past his minion to freedom.

Oswald was.

Trapped

There was only one thing left to do. So Oswald did it.

59

The Last Bit But One

It was the easiest arrest the police had ever made: all they had to do was sit outside the jewel room, drinking tea, and waiting for Stig to go down.

The hardest part was trying to drink tea through a gas mask.

Two days and 357 cups of tea later, Stig was finally back to normal size.

Stig and Bingly were led away.

The Last Bit

Oswald Bingly sat in the cell, thinking dark thoughts of yet another escape. Meanwhile, Stig Stubble was reading a letter from his mum.

Dunrunnin
SE 54

Dear boys,

Thank you for the luvly jewlery you sent. Don't be angry, but none of it went with my clothes so I gave it to Oxfam.

They said that the poliss had been asking about jewlery just like it — isn't that funny?

I never even knew the poliss was allowed to wear jewlery.

I told your friend Jimmy about it, but he went all nervous and shook a lot, and flew off soon after. I have not seen him since.

He took a lovely crown with him when he went. He said he wanted it to remind him of you two — wasn't that sweet?

love

Mumsy xx

63

Jimmy the crow flew to South America, where he married a toucan called Carmen who sings in night clubs.

They have two children.

Jimmy is thought to be the richest crow in the history of the world.

The End